HAVERFORD TOW
1601 DARBY RO
HAVERTOWN

Pigeon Hero!

By **Shirley Raye Redmond**

Illustrated by **Doris Ettlinger**

ALADDIN PAPERBACKS

New York London Toronto Sydney Singapore

For my sister, Sandy Hagen—S. R. R.
To Gail Wood Miller—D. E.

A special thank you to the U. S. Army Communications-Electronics Museum,
Fort Monmouth, New Jersey.

First Aladdin edition November 2003

Text copyright © 2003 by Shirley Raye Redmond
Illustrations copyright © 2003 by Doris Ettlinger

ALADDIN PAPERBACKS
An imprint of Simon & Schuster Children's Publishing Division
1230 Avenue of the Americas, New York, NY 10020

All rights reserved, including the right of reproduction in whole
or in part in any form.

READY-TO-READ is a registered trademark of Simon & Schuster.

Book design by Debra Sfetsios
The text of this book was set in Century Oldstyle.

Printed in the United States of America
2 4 6 8 10 9 7 5 3 1

This book has been cataloged with the Library of Congress: 2002008842
ISBN 0-689-85486-2 (Aladdin pbk.)
ISBN 0-689-85487-0 (Aladdin Library edition)

Pigeon Hero!

By **Shirley Raye Redmond**

Illustrated by **Doris Ettlinger**

This is a true story
about a pigeon.
His name was G. I. Joe.
He was a carrier pigeon
in World War II.

One day

the British Fifty-sixth Brigade

marched into a town

in Italy.

The soldiers were ready

for a big battle.

American war planes

were coming to help them.

But the Germans fled.
The people in the town
did not want to fight.
The soldiers took over
the town peacefully.

Then the soldiers
suddenly remembered.
Warplanes were coming!
The planes would bomb the town.

What could they do?

The planes would come soon.

Many people would die.

One soldier tried to send

a radio message,

but the radio was broken.

The telegraph lines

were down too.

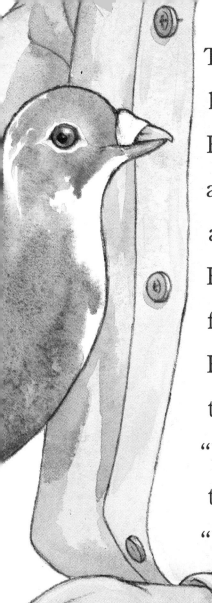

Then the soldier
looked at G. I. Joe.
He quickly wrote
a message
and put it in a small tube.
He took G. I. Joe
from his cage.
He tied the tube
to the bird's leg.
"Fly, Joe!"
the soldier shouted.
"Fly as fast as you can!"

G. I. Joe knew what to do.

He was a military pigeon.

He was brave.

He flew high into the sky.

G. I. Joe flew fast.

Flap, flap, flap.

G. I. Joe heard
machine gun fire.
The enemy below
was shooting at him!

They did not want Joe

to carry his important message.

But G. I. Joe was not afraid.

He flew higher.

Flap, flap, flap.

Then G. I. Joe saw a hawk.

The hawk wanted to eat Joe!

But G. I. Joe was smart.

He flew down, down, down.

He flew to the left,

and then he flew to the right.

Flap, flap, flap.

The hawk did not catch him.

The sky grew dark.

It began to rain.

G. I. Joe was not afraid.

He could fly

in bad weather.

Flap, flap, flap.

He would not get lost.

Back in the town

the troops watched the sky.

They were worried.

The people were worried too.

What if G. I. Joe

did not make it in time?

What if the war planes

were on the way?

At last G. I. Joe arrived
at the American air base.
The pilots were on the runway.
An airman picked up the pigeon.
He quickly read the note.
Then he signaled the control tower.
The bombing raid was called off—
just in time!

G. I. Joe had saved the day!

The airman sent the pigeon

back to the British troops.

This time Joe carried

a new message.

The planes would not come!

The town was safe.

The soldiers cheered.

The people cheered too.

G. I. Joe was a hero!

When the war was over,

G. I. Joe went to London.

The Lord Mayor of London

gave Joe a medal.

Then G. I. Joe went to live

at a zoo in Detroit.

Many people came

to see the famous

war veteran with feathers!

Author's Note

G. I. Joe was just one
of many brave war pigeons.
They flew across stormy seas
with messages from
submarines and battleships.
They were trained to fly at night.
They flew over enemy lines.
Small cameras tied around the birds
took secret photos.
These pigeons did many
amazing things!